By the same author:

Bradley and the Magic Carpet

Bradley Trouve un Dinosaure (French edition)

2nd print edition © 2019

Text copyright © Julian Hilton 2013
Illustration copyright © Jacqueline East 2013 from
concepts by Julian Hilton

ISBN 978-1-9164-6152-9

Singing Frog Publishing

www.singingfrogpublishing.com

Find us on Facebook and Instagram
(#singingfrogpublishing)

Bradley and the Dinosaur

by

Julian Hilton and Jacqueline East

...for my magical nephew and with thanks to all those who made this possible...

Bradley's Mum needed flowers for the table.

So he ran into the garden
as fast as he was able.

Picking one here, taking two there.

Bradley found flowers everywhere.

Just after he'd seen the very best one,
a noise made him jump
and the flower was

GONE!!

As Bradley spun around to see,
he fell down upon his hands and knees.

He listened again and suddenly heard
a scratching and a rustling.

Was it a bird?

This noise was bigger,
much bigger than that!
Was it a mongoose?
Or even a cat?

A humungous head on a long spotty neck
Came into the garden. It stretched and it
stretched and it
STRETCHED!

At last there followed a pair of shoulders
and two stubby legs as big as

BOULDERS

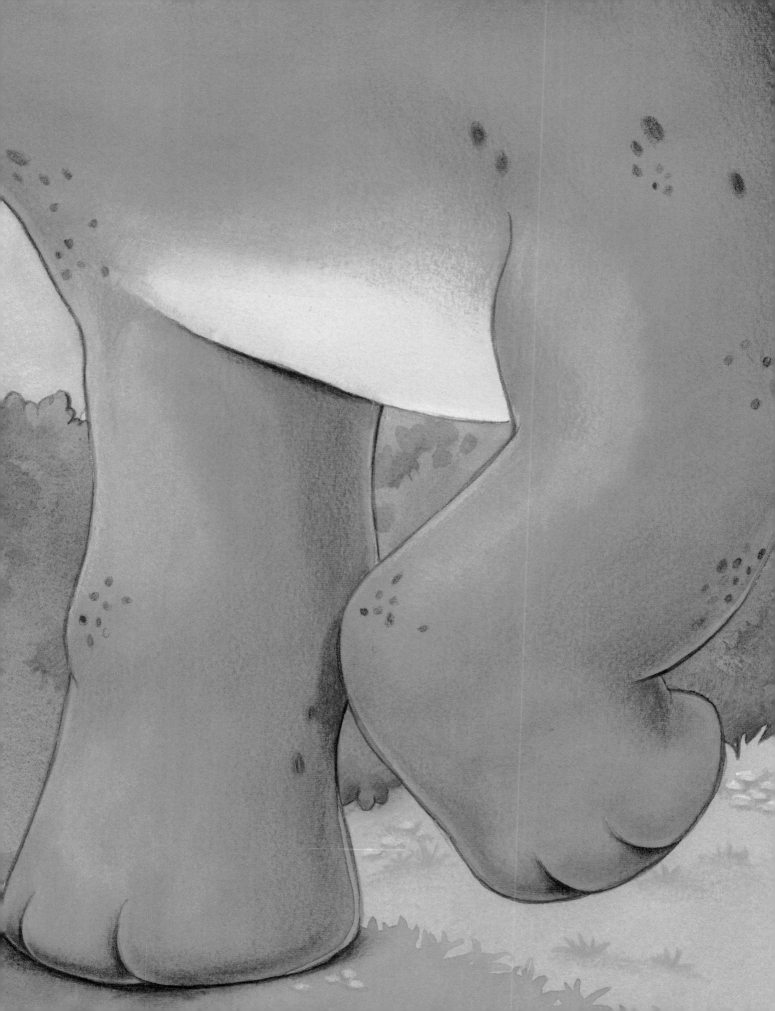

ON and ON the creature appeared...

With a giganormous tail that tickled Bradley's ear!

He thought about just what he should do
then offered the creature a daisy or two.

The Monster munched,
then started to roar.
Bradley had discovered a

DINOSAUR!

Not scary or ferocious, terrifying or wild.
This dinosaur seemed to be fond of the child...

As it gave a call and turned about
Bradley grabbed onto the tail it held out.

The dinosaur jumped
into a very dark hole...

...and disappeared. POP!
Just like a mole.

Then came a tunnel as long as his friend.
Longer in fact - it went on without end.

When at last they came out of
that space, guess
what he saw?

...All over the place !

There were ploddy Plodicuses, stumpy Sauruses and dinky Doyouthinkysauruses.

Tumbling Pterydactyls, soaring Sauropods ...and sawing Sauruses.

What an amazing sight!
He slid down a tail and
roared with delight.

He flew in the air and saw all around
the wonderful sight that was...

Dinoland!

He was so happy
he gave them all
flowers.

...He didn't want to leave,
but he'd been there
for hours...

Hardly keeping awake,
Bradley said goodbye and got
back to the tunnel with the
help of a fly.

"Bradley ! Where are you?", his Mum called out.

He zoomed up the garden...
"I'm coming!! Don't shout!"

"Where are the flowers, my little explorer?"

"I gave them to the dinosaurs,
I've got none left over."

"Oh that's so kind! Come inside for your tea.
I've made you your favourite..."

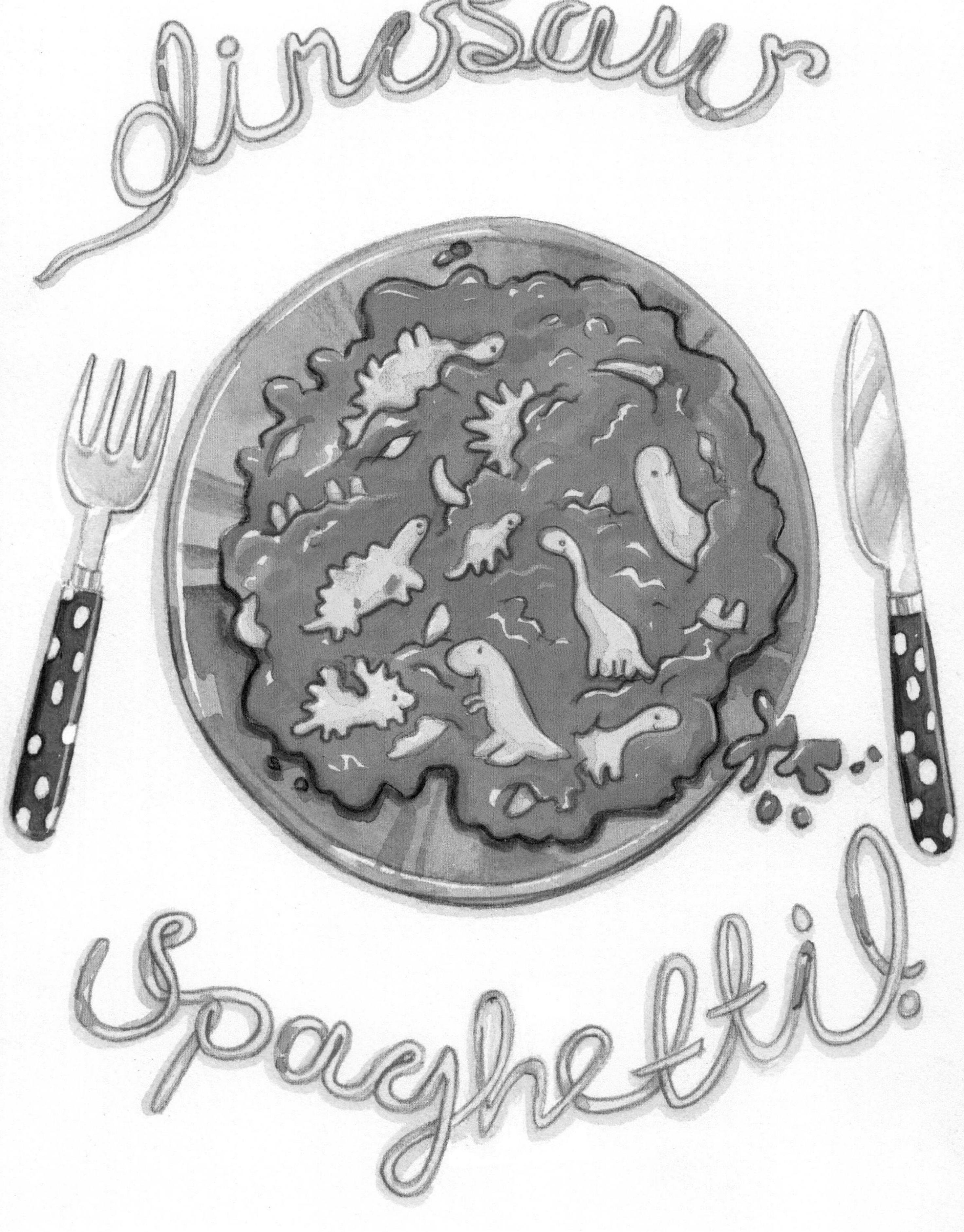
dinosaur
spaghetti!

And as Bradley went to bed
he counted *Dinosaurs*
instead.

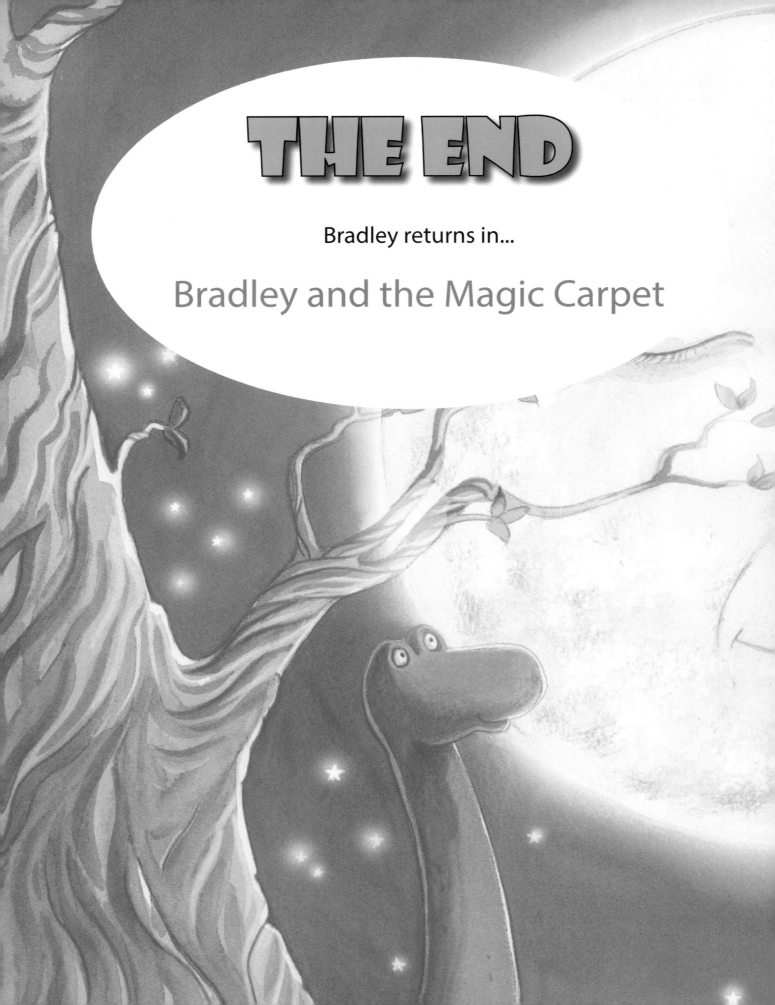

THE END

Bradley returns in...

Bradley and the Magic Carpet

Printed in Great Britain
by Amazon